DETECTIVE Zack

Red Hat Mystery

Illustrated by
Lad Odell

Written by
Jerry D. Thomas

DETECTIVE Zack

Red Hat Mystery

Camp Aug 9/07

Jessica
The Lord is my shepherd
Psalm 23:1

Roses are red.
Violets are blue
I walk fast
But you are faster love K.

Written by
Jerry D. Thomas

Illustrated by
Lad Odell

A Faith Building Guide can be found on page 120.

Faith Building Guide
Ages
9 and up

Faith Kids® is an imprint of
Cook Communications Ministries, Colorado Springs, CO 80918
Cook Communications, Paris, Ontario
Kingsway Communications, Eastbourne, England

DETECTIVE ZACK: THE RED HAT MYSTERY
© 2002 by Jerry D. Thomas

First Printing, 1992 (Pacific Press)
First Faith Kids® Printing, 2002
Printed in the United States of America
1 2 3 4 5 6 7 8 9 10 Printing/Year 06 05 04 03 02

Edited by: Heather Gemmen
Designed by: Big Mouth Bass Design, Inc.
Cover Illustrated by: Lad Odell

Library of Congress Cataloging-in-Publication Data

Thomas, Jerry D., 1959-
   Detective Zack: red hat mystery / written by Jerry D. Thomas ;
illustrated by Lad Odell.
   -- (Detective Zack ; 5)
Summary: As ten-year-old Zack continues his travels with an archeologist
through the Middle East, he looks for further clues to support the
stories from the Bible.
   ISBN 0-7814-3802-0
   [1. Bible--Antiquities--Fiction. 2. Christian life--Fiction.] I. Odell, Lad ill. II.
Title.
   PZ7.T366954 Dfg 2002
   [Fic]--dc21
                                    2001004331

Dedication

To Katherine,
Who always believes I can,
but doesn't realize she is the reason why.
Without her I would be lost,
not just in writing, but in life.

And on the way home from the airport.

Note to Parents and Teachers

The archeological information in this book is accurate, but it is not intended to be precise or complete. It is intended to be simple enough for young minds to understand.

Also, the sequence of sites visited on this trip may not follow the normal, logical route of a common tourist. Instead, the sites and experiences are arranged in such a way as to appeal to the logic and interest of young minds intent on following their heroes of the Bible.

Books in this Series

Contents

ONE

Trouble at King Tut's Tomb

Somewhere in Egypt

Have you ever watched popcorn being popped in a hot air popper? You know, the little kernels get blown all around, bouncing off the popper's walls, getting hotter and hotter until they explode into popcorn.

Today, I feel a lot like popcorn. If it gets any hotter in this car, or if I bounce off the ceiling one more time, I may explode into popcorn myself.

And let me tell you, it's not easy to write when you're being treated like popcorn. But it could be worse. We could be walking. Or riding camels.

I'm not really complaining. Everyone else back home started school last week. I get to start late because Dad thought I could learn a lot here. And since my dad and I started on this trip with Dr. Doone, I've seen a lot of really interesting things.

Dr. Doone is an archeologist (ark-e-all-o-jist). That means he studies old things—old cities, old books or writing, broken pottery and jars, bones, anything that's left from people long ago. He's been over here to Egypt and Israel many times.

But on this trip, he's not digging up old tablets or bones or jars. He's making a video about Bible places and things. He invited my dad and me to go along and help with the cameras and lights and stuff.

But I'm here for another reason too. Since our family trip last summer, Dad has been calling me "Detective Zack." It was my job on that trip to look for clues that showed that Noah's Flood really happened. We found a lot of good scientific clues and I believe Noah's Flood was real.

And now I'm "Detective Zack" again. Like Dad told me, some people don't believe the stories in the Bible. They think those stories are all just stories—like fairy tales, myths, or legends. So I'm hunting down clues that show that people really lived just like those stories said. If the clues show that people once lived like the Bible says, then the Bible stories really happened to real people.

I've already filled one notebook with clues. I saw people who still live today almost like Abraham lived in his day. I saw a well just like the one Joseph was thrown in by his brothers (it might have even been the same one). One clay tablet told about a man who traded his birthright for three sheep. Doesn't that sound a lot like the Bible story of Esau trading his birthright to Jacob for a bowl of beans?

And my friend Achmed (Ock-med) and I got to dig for clues at the site where Dr. Doone thinks the city of Sodom was destroyed by fire from heaven. And Ach showed me how to ride a camel. (I call him "Ach." He calls me "Zock.")

So this is my second notebook of clues. And already, so many things have happened that I haven't had time to write it all down. Right now, we are bouncing through the desert on our way out of Egypt. We're headed to Mt. Sinai next, where God gave Moses the Ten Commandments.

Dr. Doone arranged for us to join a special caravan to Mt. Sinai that would follow the same route the Israelites took when they left Egypt with Moses. We are now flying across the sand toward the Red Sea in a group of taxi-cars.

We're not really flying, even thought the drivers seem to be trying to go fast enough to take off. And we are on a road, not the sand, but at this speed the bumps send me bouncing off the ceiling and walls.

So if I can hold on to my notebook and pencil, I'll tell you about Egypt. And believe me, some strange things are happening. After we saw the pyramids and the

Sphinx, Dr. Doone took us to see the tomb of King Tutankhamen (too-tan-com-men). Everyone thinks his name was too long, so they just call him King Tut. And guess who else I saw there. The man in the red hat!

I had seen that same man watching us at the pyramids and on our boat trip on the Nile River. I thought then that he was acting suspicious. Now I am sure of it. He was definitely following us at King Tut's tomb. I saw him duck around a corner ahead of us, so I started to sneak after him.

"Zack," Dr. Doone called me back, "archeologists have uncovered many tombs of Egyptian kings. Even the pyramids were tombs. But they had all been robbed of their treasures. Only King Tut's tomb has been found with all the treasure still inside."

"How much treasure was there?" I asked, looking around for that red hat to reappear.

"More than 2,200 objects were found there—crowns, statues, jewelry, and stuff. And it is worth more than twelve million dollars!"

"Wow," I said. "King Tut must have really been an important king."

Dr. Doone laughed. "No, King Tut was only ten years old when he became king. And he only lived eight more years."

"He wasn't much older than me." I was amazed.

"Yes. And since he didn't live long, he wasn't a very important king. Imagine what kind of treasures were in the tombs of the kings who ruled for forty or fifty years, the ones who built the pyramids and won battles with their armies. But all those treasures are lost now."

After Dr. Doone had shown us around the tomb area and told about King Tut's treasures which were now in a museum, I took some pictures with my camera. Then Dad called me.

"Zack, you're going to set that camera down and lose it. Where is your camera bag?"

I looked blank for a second. My camera just fit inside its neat little black case with a zipper. "Oh, I know. It's still in the video camera bag. I've been leaving it there so I wouldn't lose it."

Dad opened the big black bag and reached down past the video camera. "Here it is. And somewhere in here I have an extra camera strap." He rummaged through the bag again and pulled out the strap. "This snaps right onto your little camera bag. Now, just hang it around your neck, and you won't lose the camera or the case."

Since I was there, I decided to tell Dad about the man in the red hat. "Dad, someone is following us."

Dad just looked at me. "What are you talking about?"

I tried to explain. "Back at the pyramids, I saw this man looking at us. Later I saw him following us toward our hotel. Then he was on the boat we were on. And now . . ."

"Whoa!" Dad put his hands on my shoulders while he spoke. "You're talking too fast. Who is this person that goes everywhere we do? Slow down and start over, Zack."

I took a deep breath. "Back at the pyramids . . ."

"Zack," Dr. Doone called from behind me. "There's someone here I want you to meet. He has some questions for you."

I turned and my mouth fell open. The man with Dr. Doone was the man with the red hat!

Discoveries and Clues

Words to Remember

Archeologist: Someone who studies old things—old cities, old books or writing, broken pottery and jars, bones, anything that's left from people long ago

King Tutankhamen (King Tut): A boy who was king of Egypt. His tomb was filled with treasure.

Important Facts

After the important facts I found about Abraham, Jacob and Esau, Joseph, and the burning of Sodom, I'm ready to look for more.

Clues from an Old Letter

In the car (still!)

Zack, this man would like to meet you," Dr. Doone said. "His name is Mitchell Roberts."

The man in the red hat took off his hat and stuck out his hand. "Pleased to meet you, Zack."

His hand felt cold and clammy. "N-n-nice to meet you, Mr. Roberts," I said. I stared as Dr. Doone introduced him to my dad. He looked normal enough. His black hair and white teeth matched his black pants and white shirt. Even his big black boots matched. He seemed a little older than my dad. They turned back toward me.

"Zack," Dr. Doone said, "Mr. Roberts doesn't believe the stories in the Bible. I told him that you are our detective and that you keep the evidence that the Bible stories are about real people."

I nodded and Mr. Roberts said, "I know what the

Bible says. It just can't be real, that's all. I mean, think of what was in this tomb. All the riches and power of Egypt was controlled by the pharaoh. But the Bible says that Moses turned away from a chance to be Pharaoh just so he could lead a bunch of slaves to a new land. No one would make a dumb choice like that."

I hadn't thought of that. One of these rich, treasure-filled tombs could have belonged to Moses. He could have been a powerful pharaoh. He could have been as famous as King Tut. But...

"I don't think it was a dumb choice," I said. "After all the riches he had, King Tut is just a mummy today. But I believe Moses is living in heaven today. After all, he and Elijah came down and talked to Jesus while he was on earth. It seems like a pretty good choice to me."

Mr. Roberts looked surprised. "I guess you have a point there, if you really believe the Bible is true. Maybe I should hang around and learn more."

The next thing I knew, Mr. Roberts had decided to join our tour group to Mt. Sinai. I guess I should be glad that he wants to know more about the Bible. But I'm still not sure I trust him. I'd better keep my eyes open. I wish Ach was here to help.

There are about thirty people in our group now, riding in twelve different cars. I think I saw a girl about my age get into one of the cars before we left.

As we rode along, Dr. Doone had some more interesting information for me. "Do you remember why it is so hard to find evidence about Bible people and places today, Zack?"

I knew that answer. "Because it all happened so long ago." I pulled out the string with knots that Dr. Doone made for me at the beginning of our trip. He colored the knots to help me remember. And on this string, the distance between each knot stands for five hundred years.

The first knot on the string stands for today. It's yellow. The next one down is blue and it stands for the time Christopher Columbus discovered America. Everything you ever learned about American history— George Washington, Daniel Boone, Abraham Lincoln, everything—happened in the five hundred years between those two knots.

Then we skip down past two knots with no color to the big knot right in the middle of the string. It's red and stands for the time that Jesus lived here. That was one thousand five hundred years before Columbus.

The next knot down is purple and it stands for the time of Daniel—you know, with the lions' den and everything. The brown knot under that one stands for King David's time. And five hundred years before David is

Moses, with the pink knot. The last knot is black and it stands for Abraham's time.

So if you look at my string and all its colored knots, you can see how long ago everything happened. You can understand why it's hard to find out much about the people who lived way back then.

"Right," Dr. Doone said. "Now, Zack, as you know, we have found many clay tablets and stone walls in Egypt that tell us what life was like in those days."

"And in Egypt," I reminded him, "it is written in hieroglyphics (hi-row-glif-icks), that funny looking Egyptian picture writing."

"That's right," he agreed and smiled. I guess he was happy that I remembered something that he had told me. A good detective remembers everything!

"Well," he continued, "thanks to King Tut's father-in-law, we have written evidence that tells the same story as the Bible."

"Wait a minute," I said. "This is confusing. Who was King Tut's father-in-law and what Bible story did he write about?"

Dr. Doone explained. "King Tut was married, even though he was very young. His wife's father was Akhenaton (ack-hen-a-tawn), a pharaoh famous for changing the religion of the Egyptians. He wanted all the

Egyptians to worship only the sun-god instead of the river-god and the bull-god and the cat-god and all their other gods."

I just looked at him. These Egyptians were very confusing.

He hurried on. "But all that's not important right now. At the time Akhenaton ruled, Egypt controlled the land of Canaan that Moses had led the children of Israel to."

"So the people who lived in Canaan were ruled by the pharaoh?"

"Well, he didn't really tell them what to do. His armies came by and collected money from them every few years. And they expected the pharaoh to protect them from other armies. Well, about a hundred years ago, an old woman digging in the ruins of Akhenaton's city found some clay tablets. Archeologists now believe that those tablets are letters from some of the kings in Canaan to Akhenaton."

I nodded and kept listening.

"These letters ask Akhenaton to send help," Dr. Doone continued. "The kings say that a new tribe of people were taking over the land. They called these people 'Hebrews.'"

"Hebrews? Who were they?"

Dr. Doone explained. "The people who followed Moses out of Egypt called themselves Israelites. But the people of other countries called them Hebrews."

I was amazed. "Do you mean that the people who they wrote to Akhenaton about were the Israelites?"

Dr. Doone nodded and smiled.

"So when the walls of Jericho fell down and the Israelites were taking over all the other cities, the Canaanites wrote to King Tut's father-in-law and said, 'Help!'"

Dr. Doone said, "It's one of the earliest written evidence we have where a story from the Bible is supported by a writer from another country."

"That's an important clue that the Bible stories are true," I agreed, writing it all down in my notebook.

It was only a few minutes later that I noticed the car slowing down. The other cars in front of us were stopping. "What's going on?" I asked.

"It looks like we're been stopped by some police or soldiers," Dad said. I leaned out the window to see. Up ahead, men in uniforms were asking the people to get out of their cars. And everyone was getting out. And I could see why. The soldiers were holding machine guns!

I'll write more later. I hope.

Discoveries and Clues

Words to Remember

Akhenaton: King Tut's father-in-law; a famous pharaoh

Hebrews: What other tribes and countries called the Israelites

Hieroglyphics: Egyptian picture writing

Important Facts

Moses gave up the chance to be a pharaoh, so he lost out on a lot of riches. But today, he's in heaven and King Tut is just a mummy.

Clay tablet letters, written to Akhenaton from some kings in Canaan, ask for help to defeat the Hebrews. That fits the Bible story.

THREE

The Red Sea Isn't Red

By the Red Sea

The policeman tapped on the window with the barrel of his machine gun. Dr. Doone rolled down the window and spoke to him. Soon he turned to us and explained. "These are the Egyptian border police. They are inspecting all the cars leaving the country."

"What are they looking for?" I asked, still staring at the big gun.

"There are people who come to Egypt to steal artifacts. You remember, Zack, that artifacts are things archeologists find when they dig at the sites of old cities or buildings."

"Right," I said. "Artifacts can be old jars, or jewels, or statues, or anything like that."

Dr. Doone went on. "Most of these artifacts are very valuable. People who collect old objects might pay thousands and thousands of dollars for them. Naturally, the Egyptians want to keep these treasures in Egypt. Archeologists work with them by keeping their findings in Egyptian museums."

"But some people try to steal the treasures and take them out of the country," I said. Now I understood.

"A statue of a golden cat, about as big as your thumb, was stolen away from an archeological site recently," Dr, Doone added. "The police believe that a band of thieves are trying to get it out of the country. They know most of these thieves and they know how to spot people who are hiding things."

The policeman was looking at us while Dr. Doone spoke. I smiled and tried not to look guilty. Dr. Doone kept talking.

"So they are stopping all cars and all people leaving the country. We can get out of the car and stretch if we want, but we need to stay close."

I was standing around, staring at the police, when someone slapped me lightly on the back. "Zack, isn't this exciting?" I turned and stared at the man for a minute before I recognized him. It was the man with the red hat, Mr. Roberts. But now he wasn't wearing the red hat.

I watched him closely as he went over to talk to Dr.

Doone. He had his camera around his neck and his sunglasses on, so he looked like any of the other tourists. But there was something strange about him. Anyway, before long we were on our way again. I guess they didn't find the thieves or the golden cat statue.

I'm writing this by the light of the lantern in our tent. The whole group is camping by the shores of the Red Sea. I just came back from talking to Stefanie and Dr. Doone. Did I mention Stef?

I was sitting out on the sand, looking out over the waters and waiting for Dr. Doone when he came up behind me. "Zack, my friend, how are you this evening?" he asked.

"Fine," I answered. "But I have a question. The Red Sea isn't red," I said, pointing to the blue water. "So why do they call it the Red Sea?"

"I can tell you," a voice from behind me said. I twisted my neck around and saw that girl from one of the other cars in our group.

"Zack, this is Stefanie. She's traveling with her mom and dad on this tour. They're from England. I told her that you are the detective on this case."

Stefanie wasn't shy. She plopped down on the sand beside me. "Hi. Call me Stef. What's a detective doing in the desert?"

"Well, uh, hi, Stef. I guess I'm here because a lot of

people don't believe that the stories in the Bible really happened. I want to find clues to show that the Bible stories are true, that people lived just like the Bible says they did."

"Are you really finding clues and stuff?"

"We've found a whole bunch of clues. But we've been to a lot of places." I told her about some of the things I'd seen.

I noticed while she was listening, the wind kept blowing her hair down into her eyes. Every time her hair came in front of her, she pushed out her lower lip and poof, blew it back.

"So I keep it all written down in my notebook," I said. "I'm amazed sometimes that all these clues are out here, but no one talks about them."

"Perhaps I could see your notebook sometime," Stef said. "What kind of clue are you looking for here?"

We both looked at Dr. Doone. "Did you bring your Bible with you, Zack?" he asked.

I pulled it out of my backpack. "Just like you told me to," I answered. "Where do I look?"

"The book of Numbers, chapter thirty-three," he said as he leaned back in the sand. Stef reached over to help me find the right page. "Read verses ten and eleven. Remember that this is the story of the Israelites after they left Egypt and crossed the Red Sea. Now they are moving toward Mt. Sinai, like we are. Read the verses."

I read, "They left Elim and camped near the Red Sea. They left the Red Sea and camped in the Desert of Sin." I looked at Stef and she shrugged her shoulders.

"So what does it mean?" she asked.

Dr. Doone sat up. "Remember that there were more than a hundred thousand Israelites, plus their herds and animals. It would have taken a big space for them to set up camp in."

"So?"

"So we passed Elim this morning. Tomorrow we head away from the Red Sea into the desert." He waited to let us think.

Finally the answer hit me. I opened my mouth, but Stef started talking first.

"This is where they camped! Right here in the same place we're camping." The wind blew her hair in her face. With a poof, she blew it back.

Dr. Doone nodded. "This is the only spot, by the Red Sea and between Elim and the Desert of Sin, large enough to hold them all. They must have camped right here."

I turned to Stef. "Now, see, that's a clue. When you can see that a place the Bible talks about is really there,

then that's a clue that the Bible story really happened."
As I talked, I noticed Mr. Roberts, with his red hat, walking away from the camp.

"Dr. Doone, where is he going?" I asked, pointing to Mr. Roberts. Dr. Doone and Stef turned to look.

"For a walk, I guess." Dr. Doone looked puzzled. "I don't know where he could be going, but I guess that's his business."

I took a deep breath. "Don't you think there's something a little strange about him? I mean, why is he on this trip?"

Stef turned quickly and stared at me.

Dr. Doone looked skeptical. "Now, Zack, maybe he's just curious. He seems like a nice person." He stood up to leave. "Don't stay out here too late. Snakes will be out more after dark."

As he walked away, Stef turned to me and said, "What makes you think that man is strange?"

I told her about seeing him three times in Egypt, and how he just happened to be at King Tut's tomb the same time we were. "Then he decided to join us on our trip to Mt. Sinai. And he acts strange, you know, suspicious." I looked in the direction he had been walking. He was gone. "See! Now he's disappeared, right in front of us."

Stef frowned and poofed her hair back. "You know, I did see him do something strange too. Doesn't he always wear that red hat?"

"Yes."

"Well, when we were stopped by the Egyptian police, he walked over to the car you were in…"

"Right," I interrupted. "He stood there with us while the police went by."

Stef went on. "But when he walked over to your car, he took off that red hat and put it inside the car on the back seat."

My mouth fell open. "That's right! I noticed that he didn't have the red hat on when the police went by. Why would he do that? Unless…"

Stef was thinking the same thing. "Unless he was hiding something from them. Maybe he stole that artifact, that statue they were looking for."

"Maybe he hid it in his hat," I finished the thought for her. "That way, if it was found, we would be blamed instead of him." I stared at Stef and she stared at me. Then we both turned and stared out to where we had last seen the mysterious Mr. Roberts.

Discoveries and Clues

Words to Remember

Artifacts: Pottery, jars, jewels, statues, bones, anything old that an archeologist finds when an old city is dug up

Important Facts

There is a wide open spot near the Red Sea, just like it says in Numbers 33:10, 11. We camped there.

MRH (Man in Red Hat) Clues

He followed us in Egypt.

He put his red hat in our car when the police were searching for a stolen Egyptian artifact.

—— FOUR ——

God's Footprints

On the road from Mt. Sinai

I knew I forgot something. I forgot to tell you why they call it the Red Sea when it isn't red. Stef told me.

"Most people think it got its name from the rocks. They're kind of pinkish red, as you can see. So when you see their reflection in the water, or see the rocks on the bottom through the water, the sea looks red."

"OK," I said, "but…"

She went on. "Some people think it was named after a tribe of people who lived in this area, the Edomites, whose name means red."

"Alright," I tried to say, "but…"

She didn't stop. "And some people think the name was once 'the Reed Sea' because the shallow end in the north is filled with reeds. Then over the years, it got confused and written down as the 'Red Sea.'"

"I understand," I said quickly. But not quickly enough.

"Still," she said with a smile, "no one knows for sure." Then she just looked at me. "Well, what do you think?"

I waited for a second, then spoke quickly. "How did you find out about all that?"

She raised her eyebrows and poofed her hair back. "A person doesn't have to be a detective or a boy to find out some things." With that, she flipped her hair at me and ran off.

Girls. Who can understand them? Who knows if she was even right?

We've been traveling for two days to get back to Israel. I know you don't want to hear about hot, dusty car rides through the desert, so I'll tell you about Mt. Sinai.

We helped Dr. Doone set up his cameras at the bottom of Mt. Sinai. Today they call it the "Mountain of Moses." We were in front of an old church and some buildings Dr. Doone called a monastery. He said some people thought they could be more holy if they came and lived there at a holy place. There was also a library/museum for artifacts, especially old copies of Scriptures.

When we got the lights just right, Dr. Doone started his talk. "People in this area have long believed that this is the mountain Moses climbed to receive the Ten Commandments from God. The children of Israel would have been camped in the big open plain here in front of us, and Moses would have climbed up here," he pointed to the trail going up, "to meet with God."

I looked up and tried to imagine the whole mountain shaking with thunder and lightning and God's voice. It was enough to make you shiver in the hot sun.

Dr. Doone went on. "If God left marks behind when he had contact with the earth, then this mountain would be covered by his footprints."

We started up the trail past the monastery, but had to stop by a scraggly looking bush. As other people began to photograph the bush, I looked at Dad and Dr. Doone. Dad just shrugged his shoulders.

"No," Dr. Doone laughed, "We don't want to film this bush."

"Then why are all these people taking pictures of it?" I asked.

"Well, Zack, remember that Moses herded sheep in this same area before God sent him back to Egypt to free his people. Well, according to some traditions, this very bush is the burning bush that God spoke to Moses through."

I leaned out past one person and stared at the bush. It looked old and dusty, but not like it had been on fire. "It doesn't look very special. How could anyone tell if it was the same bush?"

Dr. Doone smiled. "That's exactly the problem, Zack. I can believe that people would remember the right mountain, and tell their children and grandchildren about it. A mountain is easy to describe and remember. But a bush is different. And Moses was the only one who saw it burning anyway."

"Even if this isn't Moses' burning bush," I said, finally standing right in front of it, "it's kind of amazing to imagine that Moses stood here and talked to God. And that God talked to him."

Dad nodded his head. "That is what's amazing about this whole mountain."

We hiked up the trail and saw the place where some people think Moses hid so God could walk by (read about it in Exodus 33:18–23), and the cave that Elijah hid in. You probably forgot that Elijah was even at Mt. Sinai, didn't you? I did. But this is where he ran to hide from Queen Jezebel (read about it in 1 Kings 19:1–9).

On the way back down, I walked with Dad. "Zack, zip up your camera case tighter. This dust is probably getting in it."

I pulled on the zipper again. "The zipper is stuck or something. I can't get it to zip up right." I gave up. The wind was blowing and dust kept getting in my eyes.

"Oww! Too bad God really didn't leave footprints up here," I said, trying not to think about the dust. "That would be even more amazing than dinosaur footprints."

He laughed. "Well, at least we know that God isn't extinct. But you know, in a way, God did leave his footprints here."

I squinted at him. "What do you mean?"

"We think of footprints as evidence that something or someone has been here. We don't find the evidence that God was here by looking in the sand. We find it by looking at people."

"You mean God left his footprints on people?"

Dad started to smile, but the dust got in his mouth. With his hand over his mouth, he said. "Where can you find evidence that God really was on this mountain, Detective? By looking in the sand or in the bushes?"

I shook my head.

"No you can't," he agreed. "The best evidence that God was really here is in the people who were here. They were changed because they met God. The words God spoke here and the instructions Moses wrote down was the beginning of a new relationship between God and his people."

I thought about that. "So one of the clues that the story of Mt. Sinai is true is what happened to the people who were there. They changed, so something must have happened."

"They didn't change immediately," Dad added. "But God began to teach them how to live and be happy."

By now we were near the bottom. From a distance, I could see Stef running to meet us. "Zack, come quick!" she shouted. The wind was twirling her hair so that it looked like dancing snakes on her head. Dad smiled and headed toward the monastery.

I ran down to meet Stef. "What is it?" I asked.

She coughed up some dust and tried to breathe through all that hair. "I thought I saw you at your car," she started to say. "Come on, I'll explain on the way." She turned and ran back toward the parked cars.

"What are you talking about?" I shouted, but she kept going. I ran after her. Either she was crazy, or else she knew something important. By the way, Stef was right about the Red Sea. I asked Dr. Doone.

I grabbed my hat to keep it on my head. "Wait for me!"

Discoveries and Clues

Words to Remember

Red Sea: It's not red. But they call it the Red Sea because of the red rocks, some tribes nearby, or something like that.

Mt. Sinai: Mountain of Moses

Monastery: A place where some people go to live to try to be more holy

Important Facts

Mt. Sinai is an important clue. It's here, just like the Bible says.

The best clue that God was at Mt. Sinai is the footprints he left on the people who were there. They changed because they met God.

FIVE

A Talking Donkey and a Thief

Following Balaam's trail

We stopped behind a small building near the cars and Stef started to explain. "When I was coming down the trail, I thought I saw you over at your car."

I shook my head. "It wasn't me. I was still…"

"I know that now! But when I thought I saw you, I ran down to see what you were doing. When I got closer, it wasn't you."

"Stef, we already know that. Tell me who it was."

She shook her head and poofed her hair back. "I couldn't tell who it was, but I knew something strange was going on. So I ducked down behind one car and peeked underneath until I could see someone's feet."

"Who was it? What were they doing?" I grabbed her

arm and tried to shake the answers out faster.

"I don't know. I saw you coming so I snuck away and ran to get you!"

"Let's go!" I shouted. We ran to the first of the cars and carefully crawled closer to ours. Then we ducked down and peeked underneath, just in time to see two feet go running away toward the mountain.

"There he goes," I whispered to Stef. And I had a pretty good idea who he was.

"Who was it and what was he doing?" Stef asked as we reached our car. One of the back doors was open. It was easy to see that whoever it was had been searching for something by dumping our bags out onto the floor.

"He was robbing you," Stef declared. "Let's get him."

She looked off in the direction the person had run. "How will we find him?"

I smiled and adjusted the detective hat on my head. "No problem. We'll just follow his footprints in the sand."

Stef looked impressed. We took four steps in the direction the footprints led. Then a sudden gust of wind blinded our eyes with dust.

"Oh, no," I said, even before I opened my eyes. I knew what I would see when the wind died down. Nothing. And I was right. The footprints were gone. The wind had covered them up.

That was the end of our detective work that day. We went and found Dad and showed him the car. He went through the bags and nothing seemed to be missing. "Probably just a thief, looking for something to steal. You two must have scared him off just in time."

"Did you ever see Mr. Roberts and his red hat while we hiked up the mountain?" I whispered to Stef. She shook her head.

We packed up and drove away soon after that. Our first real stop was this afternoon. When the caravan of cars stopped near a river, Dr. Doone asked us to grab the camera equipment and follow him. I guess I had been sleeping a little, so I asked Dad where we were.

"Well, we've been following the path of the Israelites on their way to the Promised Land. This must be one of the last stops along the way, because we are nearly to Israel." He grabbed the camera and I grabbed the light pack and we followed the trail.

Dr. Doone was waiting at the site where archeologists had been digging. It must have been an old city or town. He waved us up to an old wall and waited while we set up. Then he began.

"Before the Israelites crossed over the Jordan to the Promised Land, they conquered several kings and their armies. One king was so scared of them that he hired a prophet to curse this new tribe of people. Many have doubted that this prophet, Balaam, really existed."

I looked around with more interest now. The story of Balaam and his talking donkey is one of my favorites. I saw that Mr. Roberts had joined us and was listening too. I tried to watch him out of one eye while I listened.

Dr. Doone went on. "But this site has given us evidence that Balaam was a real person and that he lived in this area. The inscription on this wall refers to 'Balaam, son of Beor, prophet of the Gods.' Our next stop will be beside the fallen walls of Jericho."

Stef and I walked around for a while and watched the workers at the archeological site digging and hauling away the dirt. One of them used a donkey to carry a basket of dirt. I walked up to the donkey as it stood waiting and said, "So, seen any angels recently?"

The donkey snapped its head around and stared at me. Then he leaned toward me like he was going to whisper a secret. I leaned a little toward him and listened.

"Heeaww! Heeaww! Heeaww!" The donkey brayed right in my ear. I jumped back and tripped on a rock. When I stopped rolling, I was laying face down in the dust. I moaned and lifted my head up enough to see Stef. She was rolling in the dust too. Because she was laughing too hard to stand up!

"It wasn't that funny," I grumbled at her as I stood up and started brushing the dust off.

"You should have seen your face," she said, still laughing. She looked back up at the donkey, who was completely ignoring us. "I wonder if that's his answer to every question or if he's just tired of being asked about angels."

We were at our camp for the night when I thought I heard something outside behind the tent. It was nearly dark, so I snuck out the front and ran to Stef's tent. "Stef! Stef, come here quick!"

Her head stuck out the tent flap. "Zack? What is it?"

"Someone's outside my tent by the cars. Let's catch him this time. Come on," I whispered as I pulled her out. We dashed around to my tent again and grabbed an extra tent stake rope laying there. Then we slipped around the side by the parked cars.

"I see someone," Stef whispered, "there, by that jeep. I can't tell if it's Mr. Roberts."

"I see him. I'm not sure either. Let's get closer." We crawled past two more cars and lay on the ground beside the jeep. We could see two feet on the other side.

I whispered to Stef. "You go back and get Dad and Dr. Doone. I'm going to rope this guy."

"Zack, that could be dangerous," she whispered back.

"Why don't I get them first, and we'll let them grab him."

"Don't worry. I have a plan," I said. "Just hurry back." She crawled away and took a deep breath. I had a plan alright. I just hoped it was going to work.

I wiggled under the jeep until I was almost to the other side. The person's feet were pointed toward the jeep, like he was looking in the windows. I reached out and snaked the rope around his feet in a loop. Then I tied a quick slipknot and slid back out from under the jeep.

I stood up and jerked the rope as hard as I could. Smack! I heard him hit the sand and shout, "Hey! Help!" I kept pulling the rope and dragged him at least partway under the jeep.

"I got you this time," I shouted back. My plan was to drag him far enough under the jeep that he couldn't get up, and then hold on until Stef brought help. I figured he wouldn't be able to reach his feet to untie them and get away. At least I hoped he couldn't.

I saw the beam from a flashlight shine against the jeep and heard Stef shouting. I shouted back to her. "I've got him. Over here!"

My prisoner was banging against the jeep and shouting when she ran up with my dad, Dr. Doone, and Mr. Roberts.

Discoveries and Clues

Words to Remember

Inscription: Writing on a tablet or a wall or an artifact

Important Facts

Some people doubted that the prophet Balaam really existed. But archeologists found an inscription on a wall that mentions a prophet named Balaam.

MRH Clues

Someone tried to steal stuff from our car. We would have caught him but the wind covered the footprints.

Note: Never talk to a donkey.

SIX

The Truth About Jericho

At Jericho

For a second, I stared at Mr. Roberts. He was supposed to be the thief. He was supposed to be on the other end of my rope. But I have to admit, it was easier to pull the person I caught with my rope than I thought it would be.

"Zack, what's happening?" Dad rushed right to me. Dr. Doone and Mr. Roberts ran around to the other side of the jeep where someone was still shouting for help. It seemed like a good time to drop the rope.

Mr. Roberts reached down and pulled the person out from under the jeep. "Okay, stop shouting and start talking. Who are you and what were you doing?" he asked.

"Are you alright?" Dr. Doone asked at the same time. Meanwhile, Stef shined the light in my eyes to see if I was alright. Since that blinded me for a few seconds, I couldn't see who I had caught with my rope. Then I heard his voice.

"I was just looking for my friend Zock," the voice said. "Suddenly, I am pulled down under the jeep."

"Ach? Ach, is that you?" I raced around the jeep, and there he was. "Ach, I'm sorry. I didn't mean to trap you! I thought I was catching a thief," I said, glancing quickly at Mr. Roberts.

Mr. Roberts looked at me. "Do you know this boy?"

"This is my friend, Achmed," I said, grabbing his arm.

Dr. Doone added, "Yes, he's the son of one of our drivers. He traveled with us a few weeks ago when we were here. Achmed, it's good to see you again."

"It's good to see you, Dr. Doone. Zock, you scared me stiffly! I thought I was gone for good."

"Come on to our tent," I told him. "I'll get you something to drink."

From behind me I heard, "Ahem," followed by poof.

"Oh, Ach, I want you to meet Stef. She's been on the trip with us. Stef, this is Achmed, my friend and camel riding teacher."

"Very nice to meet you, Achmed," Stef said. "Personally, I like camels."

Ach bowed a little. "Nice to meet you, Stuf."

I tried not to laugh. Stef frowned. "No, that's Stef."

Ach smiled and nodded. "Stuf," he said again.

The next day, Ach helped me set up the lights for Dr. Doone's video at Jericho. Dad focused the camera on the modern city of Jericho first, then slowly moved it over to the site where the old city had been dug up.

Dr. Doone said, "When you travel to Jericho today, this is the city you see. But what about the Jericho of the Bible days? Did Joshua and his army really march around the city until the walls fell down?"

I looked around and tried to imagine where they might have marched.

"Archeologists have been digging at this site for a long time to try to answer that question. Remember that the city of Jericho has been rebuilt several times. But down under the layers of rebuilding, they found the city that matched the time that the Israelites came to Canaan."

Dad focused the camera on a section that had been dug away showing rocks and stuff.

Dr. Doone went on. "Here archeologists found remains of that old city's walls. And just like the story in the Bible says, those walls were laying down."

As I was writing this down in my notebook, I leaned over to Ach and whispered, "I wonder if the walls fell down because of an earthquake."

At almost the same time, Dr. Doone said, "Some see

this as evidence of an earthquake, not as a clue proving a Bible story. But I don't think that matters. God may have used an earthquake to bring the walls down when Joshua and his people shouted and blew their trumpets."

I nodded and wrote faster. It made sense.

"But the facts are that the Bible says that in Joshua's time, Jericho's walls fell down. And they did."

Ach and Stef and I explored around for a while, especially around the ancient stone tower. Then Dr. Doone called me over. "Zack, here's another clue you may want to write down."

I pulled out my notebook and pencil. "OK, I'm ready."

"In those days," he said, "a city with walls like Jericho's was very difficult to capture. Usually, an army would have to set up a siege—that is, surround the city and cut off all food supplies until the people surrendered or starved. It might takes months or years."

"So inside a city with big walls was a safe place to be," I said.

"Right. Well, archeologists have discovered here in Jericho that at the time these walls fell, there was a big supply of food in the city. So Jericho was not involved in a long siege at that time."

I thought about that. "Because if it was, there wouldn't

have been much food left."

"Correct," Dr. Doone said. "And do you remember how long Joshua's army marched around Jericho?"

"Only seven days," I answered. "So that was a very short siege. There would have been plenty of food still."

"There is one more good clue that supports that the Bible story of Jericho really happened," Dr. Doone says. "The remains of the city behind the fallen walls show evidence of being burned."

"And does the Bible say that Joshua and his army burned Jericho?" I asked. Dr. Doone just nodded. I wrote it all down and went back to tell Ach and Stef. But when I found them, they were talking to Mr. Roberts.

He was saying, "Keeping your eyes out for thieves is a good idea, but you kids need to be more careful. Especially you, Zack. That was a clever way to trap someone last night."

"I'll say," Ach interrupted. "I was trapped good."

"But Zack," Mr. Roberts went on, "if Achmed here had been a real thief, he might have had a knife or gun. He would not have been so easy to hold with a rope. You might have been hurt."

I knew he was right. Dad said the same thing to me last night and made me promise to never try to stop a thief myself. "What would a thief be looking for in our stuff, Mr. Roberts?"

He fiddled with the brim of his red hat before he answered. "Could be a lot of things, Zack. Camera, clothes, watches, anything of value. Just be careful. And if you do see anyone acting suspicious, report to me. I'll be keeping a lookout also."

After he said that, he left. Ach said, "Mr. Robbers seems like a nice man." Last night, I told Ach everything that had happened since we left Egypt. He agreed that Mr. Roberts was acting strangely when the Egyptian police were looking for that missing artifact. And he kept calling him "Mr. Robbers."

Stef tried not to laugh. She said, "I don't think we can trust him."

"But he did tell us to be careful," I said. "He told us to report anything strange to him. He could be trying to help."

Ach watched the red hat in the distance. "Maybe Mr. Robbers is trying to help us. But maybe Stuf is right. Maybe he is trying to trick us into thinking he is on our side."

Discoveries and Clues

Words to Remember

Siege: When an army surrounds a city and keeps the people from getting any food or water until they surrender or die; it usually takes a long time.

Important Facts

Even though Jericho was rebuilt many times, archeologists have found the time period of Joshua's days. And the walls of the city from those days looks like they fell down. Even if an earthquake did it, they fell at the right time.

Archeological evidence from that time shows that Jericho had a large supply of food. So the city was destroyed after a very short siege (only seven days according to the Bible). Also, the city was burned at that time, like the Bible says.

MRH Clues

The thief I caught wasn't Mr. Roberts. It wasn't even a thief. It was Ach.

Mr. Roberts warned us to be careful and to report any other suspicious people to him. Is he trying to help us or trick us?

SEVEN

Joshua's Big Footprint

In the Aijalon Valley

We left early this morning and Stef was riding with us since her parents wanted to go shopping. Ach started it when he said, "Stuf, Zock has been teaching me..."

Stef interrupted. "Stef. Not Stuf. Stef."

Ach went on. "Right. That's what I said. Stuf. Zock is teaching me the American sport, baseball."

Stef rolled her eyes and sank back against the seat, but she kept listening.

"Zock is teaching me to be the catcher and the thrower and the beater of the ball."

Stef poofed back her hair and looked at me. "What are you teaching him?"

I moaned. "He means I tried to teach him to catch and pitch and to hit the ball. I didn't do a very good job of explaining. Maybe I should have taught him football."

"Now that is a great idea," Stef said. "I like football myself."

"Football?" Ach liked it too. "I have played football many, many times. What position do you play, Stuf?"

"Usually halfback," she answered, and they started talking about what they liked about the game.

I spoke up. "I like to play quarterback or receiver." They both looked at me like I had grown a second head. "You know, quarterback, the one who throws the ball. Or receiver, the one who catches it."

Stef just stared. Ach said, "I do not understand this throwing and catching thing. We are talking about football."

Stef slapped her knee. "Oh, I know. You're talking about American football. We're talking about what you call soccer."

"Soccer? Then why are you saying football?"

Poof. "They only call it soccer in America. Everywhere else it's called football. Have you played soccer?"

I grinned. "Well, no, but I've heard a lot about it. Does the halfback in soccer run with the ball like in American football?"

Ach laughed. "No one runs with the ball. They dribble down the field or kick it to others on their team."

"They dribble? Like in basketball?"

Ach looked at Stef. "No," she said, "they dribble with their feet."

I tried to imagine trying to bounce the ball up and down with my feet while I ran down a field. "I think I have a lot to learn about your kind of football," I said.

Dr. Doone spoke up. "I hate to interrupt this sports lesson, but we have a lot to learn about Joshua today too. Zack, is your Bible handy? Let's look at Joshua 8:30."

I dug my Bible out of my backpack and found the right verse. "It says that Joshua built an altar to God on Mount Ebal (ee-ball)," I reported.

"This," Dr. Doone said, pointing to one of the hills ahead of us, "is Mount Ebal. Now where are we on our string of knots?"

I pulled out the string Dr. Doone had given me. "We're past the black knot of Abraham's time and past the pink knot of Moses but we're not up to David's time. So it's still more than a thousand years before Jesus is born." I looked up at Dr. Doone. "It's still a very long time ago."

He nodded. "Well, let's go look at what they have found on top of Mount Ebal."

We found an archeological dig going on at the top of the mountain. It was a big hole with a big stone structure of some kind being dug around. Our group, including Mr. Roberts, gathered around. "This," Dr. Doone said, "is an altar."

"Wow," I said. "I thought altars were small. This is as large as a short school bus. Is it really the one Joshua built?"

"Well, the Bible says Joshua built one here. And he would have built a big one if all the Israelites were supposed to see it from down there in the valley."

We went on and explored around while Dad set up the camera to film Dr. Doone. When they were ready, Dr. Doone said, "This altar is very strong evidence that Joshua really lived and the Bible's stories really happened. It's almost like this altar is a big footprint and it's got Joshua's name written all over it."

"And God's too," Stef whispered to me. "If Joshua was real, then God is too."

By the time we left, Stef and Ach and I were ready to eat the picnic lunch we had packed. But Dr. Doone told us to wait. He had a special place in mind for our lunch. By the time our caravan stopped, I was hungry enough to eat a camel.

"OK, so what's so special about this place?" I asked after the food was spread out and the first bite of my sandwich was happily on the way to my stomach.

"This is the Valley of Aijalon (eye-jah-lawn)," Dr. Doone said as he made his own sandwich. "Do you remember anything special about that valley?"

I looked at Ach and he shrugged his shoulders. All Stef said was "poof." I shook my head.

"Look it up in Joshua 10:12," Dr. Doone suggested. So, between bites, I found the verse.

I read, "On the day the Lord gave the Amonites over to Israel, Joshua said to the Lord in the presence of Israel: 'O Sun, stand still over Gibeon, O moon, over the Valley of Aijalon.' So the sun stood still, and the moon stopped, till the nation avenged itself on its enemies."

Stef forgot to be polite and spoke with her mouth full. "You mean this is the place where Joshua prayed and the sun and moon stopped moving?" She looked up, like she wanted to be sure the sun was moving like normal today.

"That's really amazing," I said. "I wish I could have seen that."

Suddenly, there was shouting from the parking lot. We looked up to see first one man, then another, running away from the cars toward a dry creek that led to the next town. Dad ran down ahead of us to see what was happening.

"Someone really did steal from us this time," he

reported when we got to the car. "A man broke in and grabbed one of the bags out of the trunk. When someone saw him and shouted, he ran that way." He pointed toward the dry creek bed.

"Look," I nudged Ach, "footprints. Let's follow them." We could plainly see that two different people had run in that direction. We followed on toward the small trees. Suddenly, Ach grabbed my arm.

"Look!" There, under one of the trees, was a red hat.

Discoveries and Clues

Words to Remember

Football: It means soccer, unless you are in America

Mt. Ebal: A small mountain in Israel

Valley of Aijalon: The place where Joshua prayed that the sun and moon would stand still

Important Facts

On top of Mt. Ebal, the Bible says, Joshua built an altar for all the Israelites to see. And on top of Mt. Ebal, archeologists have uncovered a stone altar as big as a school bus.

EIGHT

A Stolen Bag and a Hidden Cave

In a cave

Ach and I stared at the red hat. Stef came running up behind us. "What's going on? What did you find?"

I just pointed to the hat on the ground.

"Oh! You know what this means," she said.

"I know what it looks like," I answered. "It looks like Mr. Roberts really is the thief and his hat fell off when he was running away."

Ach picked up the hat and looked at it. "It is Mr. Robbers' hat."

"Let's take it back to Dad and Dr. Doone," I said. "Maybe they will agree that he's the thief we should be looking for." We trudged back through the sand toward the cars.

I held up the hat to show Dad. "Look what we found when we followed the footprints in the sand."

He took the hat. "This looks like Mr. Roberts' hat. I wonder how it...hey, you don't think he stole the bag, do you?" He looked at Dr. Doone.

Dr. Doone frowned. "I don't think so. He doesn't seem like that kind of person."

"Wait a minute," I said. "What about what he did when the Egyptian police stopped us? And where was he the last time someone tried to steal from our car?"

Ach smiled. "When I was robbing you, he was pulling me out from under the car."

"No, Ach, you weren't stealing. I mean the time before that. Dad, don't you see?"

"I guess not, Zack. What's this about the Egyptian police?" he asked.

I started to explain when a voice behind me said, "Well, looks like he got away."

I turned and there was Mr. Roberts! I just stared. He said, "Oh good, you found my hat. Thanks." He took the hat from Dad and went on. "Exactly what was it that was taken? It wasn't the camera bag, was it?"

Dr. Doone stared at him for a second, then turned and looked through the still-open trunk of the car. "The camera bag and the lights are still here. Zack, did you have a black bag of clothes?"

"Yes," I said. "All my clothes are in a black bag."

"Well, they may still be in a black bag, but the black bag is gone."

"What?" I went and looked through the trunk too. But he was right. That thief had stolen my clothes. "Why would someone break into our car just to steal my clothes?"

Mr. Roberts answered. "They were probably after the camera, but just took the wrong bag. I guess you were lucky."

"Lucky? I don't have any more clothes," I almost shouted.

Dad laughed. "He's right, Zack. It'll be a lot easier to buy you some new clothes than it would be to get a new video camera. And we'd have to stop our trip until we could buy a new one. We'll stop and get you some more clothes tonight."

"Great," I grumbled, "just what I wanted. I get to go shopping for clothes."

"It sounds like fun to me," Stef said. "I wish someone would steal my clothes."

Meanwhile, Mr. Roberts was snooping around the car, looking closely at everything. I whispered to Ach, "Probably trying to be sure he gets the right bag next time."

Ach shook his head. "I don't know. He sounds like

he's trying to be helping you."

Our next stop was near an oasis resort. There were swimming pools and waterfalls and lots of fancy people in fancy clothes. But when we parked, we hiked away from the resort into the hills. Some of the people in our group stayed near the resort, but Mr. Roberts and several others joined the hike.

Ach and I were taking turns carrying the camera bag for Dad. Ach was still trying to teach me how to play soccer. He said, "One player plays all over the field. This one is called..." He looked at Stef. "What do you call that one, Stuf?"

"It's Stef."

Ach raised his eyebrows. "You call the soccer player Stuf?"

"No, you call me Stef!" she almost shouted. "That soccer player is called the striker. The striker begins the game by kicking the ball and plays both defense, protecting her own goal, and offense, trying to score."

I had to laugh. "If only this striker plays the whole field, then the other players stay on their own end no matter where the ball is?"

"Yes," Ach said.

"Well, they could run down to try to score, but they don't," Stef said.

"Why not?" I asked.

"Who would protect their goal?" Stef answered.

"I thought that's what the goalie did!" Before we could go on, Dr. Doone interrupted.

He said, "Think back on the story of David in the Bible. Remember when King Saul was trying to kill David. David and his men were hiding and Saul and his army went out to hunt them down. Do you remember where David hid?"

We followed Dr. Doone up a hill and around a corner. I thought about his question. "Sometimes David hid in caves."

"Right," Dr. Doone said. "And probably in caves just like this one." With that he stepped around a corner and disappeared.

"What?" We rushed after him. That corner was the entrance to a cave! "Oh, wow!" The whole group poured in.

"This is more like it," Stef sighed. The cool, moist air did feel good after that hot, dusty hike.

I looked around the cave. Even with just the light from the opening, I could see that this was a large room. Water was dripping somewhere behind me and the room was filled with rocks of all sizes. "Do you think David hid in this cave?"

"These hills are full of caves," he answered. "But it could have been this one. Remember, he was hiding with all his men, so it would have to be a large cave."

I looked around some of the big rocks. The cave tunnel disappeared into darkness at the back. "This one looks big enough. David and his men could have been hiding way back here," I called from the back of the cave. "Saul and his army could have been up there were you are, Ach, looking around."

Ach sat down next to a big rock and just watched. Mr. Roberts wandered around near the entrance.

"I always wondered why David didn't kill Saul when he had the chance in that cave," Stef said, mostly to herself. "I mean, Saul would have killed him. And God had already said that David should be king."

This time, Dad spoke up. "I guess David believed in letting God work out his own plan."

"What do you mean?" Stef said.

Dad explained. "David knew that God had chosen him to be the next king. But just as strongly, he knew that God had chosen Saul to be the first king. When God was ready for Saul to stop being king, it would happen according to his plan, not David's."

I listened to Dad's voice echoing in the cave as I snuck around the rocks. Without making a sound, I crept closer to Ach.

Dad kept talking to Stef. "Even when something bad happened, David was willing to trust God to work it out."

I slipped around the rock Ach was sitting by. Then I crept up behind him, then grabbed his arm and shouted, "Gotcha!"

"Aiiee!" Ach shouted as he jumped up and scrambled away. Then he saw that it was me. "Zock, you scared me like a crazy man."

"Zack," Dad had rushed over to see who was being killed, "what are you trying to do?"

"I was just seeing if I could sneak up on Ach like David snuck up on King Saul. At least I didn't cut a piece out of his clothes or anything."

Ach rolled his eyes. "I was afraid something was going to cut a piece out of me."

As we made our way out of the cave, Dr. Doone asked, "Where is Mr. Roberts? Wasn't he with us in the cave?"

Right away, I was suspicious. Dad went back into the cave and called, but Mr. Roberts didn't answer.

"I guess he went back early," Dr. Doone said. "He must have had something important to do."

"Ach," I whispered, "I wonder what Mr. Roberts hurried back to do. I wonder if he wanted another chance to search through our car without us around." He looked surprised.

"You might be right," he said slowly. "Mr. Robbers might be looking for a chance to steal."

I looked at Stef. She nodded. "Let's hurry," I said to Dr. Doone.

Discoveries and Clues

Important Facts

We explored a cave that David and his men could have hidden in. And David could have snuck up on King Saul. I know. I tried it.

MRH Clues

We found his red hat when we followed the footprints of the thief. He says he was chasing the thief. Whoever it was, they stole my clothes.

NINE

The Thief Gets Away

David and Goliath Valley (Valley of Elah)

It's hard to believe I'm in the same valley where David stood up to that bully, Goliath. The little creek that runs through it is dry this time of year, but it is still full of round stones.

Anyway, yesterday when we arrived at the parking lot, we didn't see Mr. Roberts. And there was something else we didn't see. Our car.

"We parked right here," Dad said, turning and looking in all directions. Our car was the only one missing from our group.

"I'll go and call the police," Dr. Doone said with a sigh. "You ask around and find out if anyone saw or heard anything."

I followed Dad, and Ach and Stef followed me. "I notice that Mr. Roberts is not around," I said to Dad. He just looked at me.

We asked several people if they had seen anything. Most had seen nothing. But one man said, "I saw a man run by here toward those cars just a few minutes before you arrived. I didn't see him take your car."

"What did this man look like?" Dad asked.

The man thought. "Oh, he was about your size. I didn't see much else. He was moving pretty fast."

We turned to leave. Then the man remembered one more thing. "Oh, I did notice his hat. It was red."

I didn't say anything. But after we found our way to a bench to wait for Dr. Doone, Dad turned and said, "Okay, tell me why you think Mr. Roberts is our thief."

I took a deep breath. "It started when we were still in Egypt. The first day I saw him, I thought he was following us. Then he just happened to show up at King Tut's tomb when we did. And then he joined our tour."

Stef joined in. "And when the Egyptian police stopped us, I saw him hide his red hat in your car after the police went by. It was like he was trying to hide who he was."

"Or trying to hide whatever was in his hat," I added. "Remember, those officers were looking for thieves who had stolen a small golden statue of a cat. Then, at Mt. Sinai, I thought he was acting suspicious. And someone did try to break into our car there."

"But you have no reason to think it was Mr. Roberts," Dad said.

"But remember yesterday, when someone did break into our car and steal my bag. We found his red hat by the trees where the thief had disappeared," I said, and Ach nodded in agreement.

"But he said he was chasing the thief," Dad protested. "He said the thief got away."

"But if he is the thief, when he realized that he had grabbed the wrong bag, he could just toss it and return like he was trying to help." I patted the camera bag. "Whoever the thief is, he must be trying to steal this camera. So whoever stole the car probably thinks this bag is in it."

Ach added, "And Mr. Robbers was gone from us when the car was taken."

Dad looked at us. "I don't know, guys. You're doing an awful lot of guessing. Another way of looking at it is that Mr. Roberts joined us because he is curious about the truth of the Bible. And he has been very helpful in trying to stop this thief. Zack, remember how he told you to be more careful that night you trapped Achmed."

I nodded. Dad was right about that. "I still think he's the thief. And I think that in just a few minutes, after whoever stole the car realizes that the camera isn't in it, Mr. Roberts will suddenly show up here again."

Dad was quiet for a minute. Then he said, "Zack, don't you think you could be making the same mistake King Saul made when he was marching his men through this area?"

"What?"

"Saul decided that David was trying to steal the kingdom from him. So he began to hunt David down to kill him. But Saul was wrong."

I had to admit Dad was right about that. He went on.

"Even though David knew that God wanted him to be the next king, he didn't kill Saul when he had the chance. God had left his footprint on David. Even though he was sure that Saul was wrong, David decided to wait and let God deal with the king. It might be a good lesson to learn."

I looked back up at the hills where David hid from Saul. "Are you saying that even if I'm sure Mr. Roberts is the thief, that I should wait and let God deal with him?"

"I think David was always glad that he decided not to kill Saul in that cave," Dad said. Before we could go on, Dr. Doone returned.

"The police will be here soon," he said. He started to explain, but he was interrupted. By you know who.

"Hey, I hear there's been some more trouble," Mr. Roberts said as he suddenly appeared. "Did you lose everything when they stole the car?"

"Who told you the car was stolen?" I asked.

He shrugged. "Everyone is talking about it. Did you have the camera case with you?"

Dad pulled it out. "I have it. Why do you ask?"

This time he smiled. "You'll need it to go on with your trip. And I'm anxious to get going. But I guess we'll have to wait for the police to return your car."

"That may take a while," Dr. Doone said. "They didn't seem too hopeful about finding it."

"Oh, it'll probably turn up soon," Mr. Roberts said with a twist of his red hat. "Let's get a cold drink while we wait."

To make a short story even shorter, just as I thought, in a few minutes the police drove up with our car. Nothing was missing. I looked at Dad. He just shrugged his shoulders.

We left soon after that. "We're going around Jerusalem for now," Dr. Doone said. "I want to come in from the other side. Besides, there's a place I know Zack wants to see."

Of course, he was talking about this valley where David fought Goliath. When we stopped, I pulled my camera out of the bag around my neck and took some pictures. Ach rushed across the creek and up the hill. Then he posed there like he was Goliath. "Send a real man to fight me. I will kill anyone." He pounded on his chest.

"I'll fight you," I shouted back. I set my camera down on the car and ran toward him, pretending to twirl a sling. Before I even pretended to let it go, Ach fell over backwards. "Hey, I didn't throw it yet!" I shouted.

"Help! Whoa," Ach shouted as he started to roll down the hill toward me. "Look out!"

I started to jump aside and escape, but I tripped over something. It was Stef's foot. "Hey, watch out," I said as I fell over her.

"Watch out yourself," she started to say as we both sat up. Then Ach rolled over us.

Discoveries and Clues

Words to Remember

Valley of Elah: The place where David fought Goliath

Important Facts

The place where David fought Goliath is really here. And there is a creek in the valley, full of stones just perfect for a sling.

MRH Clues

Mr. Roberts disappeared, and then our car disappeared. When he returned, he was concerned about the camera bag. We had it with us.

But Dad says that maybe I'm doing what King Saul did and guessing wrong about Mr. Roberts.

— TEN —

Thinking Like a Detective

Near Jerusalem

O uch."

I just laid there and moaned. "Did anyone get the license number of the truck that hit us?"

Ach sat up. "What truck?" he asked, brushing the dirt off his face.

Stef grunted and sat up. "There's no truck, Ach. It's supposed to be funny. It's not, but it's supposed to be." Poof, her hair flew back. "Will someone tell me why I've been rolled in the dirt like a soccer ball?"

"We were just playing around like we were David and Goliath. Then Ach slipped or something." I tried to explain to Stef while I pulled a small plant out of my ear.

Ach said, "I was Goliath. But I fell down. Why didn't you get out of the way?"

"I was trying to," I said, "but she got in my way."

"I didn't know I was walking into combat," Stef said. "What do you have in that camera bag? It hit me right on the head. I'm going to have a knot."

I pulled the empty camera bag around from behind my head. "It's a good thing I set the camera down. You must have hit your head on a rock," I said, standing up. "I know I have a bruise the shape of this rock on my leg."

"You're afraid you couldn't win," Ach shouted as he jumped and ran back up the hill. "I am Goliath."

"This time I will cut off your head," I shouted as I ran after him.

Stef rolled her eyes. "Boys," she said. She headed downhill, away from us.

Later, we all sat with Dr. Doone near the dry creek. "Zack, where's your Bible? I want to show you a clue in 1 Kings 9:15."

I pulled it out and found the place. "It says that King Solomon used forced labor to build the temple and palace and stuff," I said.

"Where else does he use the forced labor to build?"

I looked back at the verse and read the ending. "He also used it to rebuild the cities of Hazor, Megiddo, and Gezer."

Dr. Doone nodded. "So if this story from the Bible really happened, we could expect to see some evidence in those three cities."

I pulled out my notebook. "So can you?"

"I wish we had time to go and see for ourselves. But I can tell you that each of those three cities show evidence of Solomon's style of building. In fact, archeologists used that verse to help them."

Poof. "How did that verse help them?" Stef asked, with her hair flying.

"When they found a gateway built by Solomon at Megiddo, they read that verse and began to dig at Hazor and Gezer. Eventually, they found Solomon's gates at both of those cities. So once again, the story in the Bible is supported by the clues left behind."

The others left while I was still writing it all down. So I'm still here by the creek and they are hiking up to the top of the ridge to see across the valley. It's a good chance for me to catch up on writing in my notebook.

I'm going to pick up some of these round stones and take them home with me. That way I'll always remember that I was really here, that this place is real. And I can give one to my little brother, Alex.

Later, on our way to Jerusalem, Ach and Stef tried to teach me more about soccer. "OK, the game starts like this," Stef said. "My team has the ball and I'm the striker. So I kick the ball and we move down toward Ach's goal."

Ach added, "My team tries to take the ball away from her. I rush at her while she is dribbling and try to steal the ball with my feet. She passes to a forward on her team."

Stef took over. "If one of his players doesn't intercept the ball, we keep going toward his goal."

"I know about interceptions," I interrupted. "If Ach intercepts, it's his ball and you line up and start over going the other way."

"No," Stef shouted, "that's football. This is soccer. If Ach intercepts, he kicks the ball toward my goal or to one of his players. Nothing stops unless the ball goes out of bounds."

"And then they bring it in and start again from that spot?" I guessed.

"No," Ach said loudly, "when the ball is out of bounds, someone must throw it in. Like this," he added, waving his arms over his head and nearly hitting Dad.

Poof. "That's right," Stef agreed, blowing her hair back. "If I kick it out of bounds, then Ach throws it back in to one of his players."

"Let me get this straight," I said. "You never touch the ball with your hands, you only kick it. Except if it goes out of bounds, then you throw it back in. Why?"

Stef threw up her hands. Ach was muttering in his own language. Dad was laughing under his breath. Stef shouted again. "It doesn't matter why! That's just how you play soccer."

Dr. Doone spoke up. "Maybe I can help by changing the subject. Right out there you can see the old road to Jerusalem." We stared out the window. You could see a wide trail through the woods. "People in David's time and in Jesus' time took that road when they went to Jerusalem," he said.

Since we were on a highway, it only took us a few more minutes to get to the city of Jerusalem. "We're going to the site of the ancient city of David. There's something I want you to see," Dr. Doone said.

Before long we pulled up to the spot and got out. Dad grabbed the video camera bag (he kept it pretty close to him these days) and I grabbed the lights. "Ach, will you get my camera? I forgot to put it back in my case." He grabbed it off the dashboard and we followed Dr. Doone.

He set up near the entrance to a tunnel. When we were ready, he started. "This is the entrance to the spring of Gihon (gee-hawn). This supply of water made the city of Jerusalem a difficult city to defeat. The walls were strong and there was plenty of water available from this spring."

"Ach, I'm thirsty," I whispered. He nodded.

Dr. Doone went on. "But before David was king, this city belonged to the Jebusites (jay-bue-sites). David wanted it for his palace, but they laughed and said that he could never take it. They said, 'Even the blind and the crippled could keep you out.'"

Dr. Doone stopped and said, "OK, let's move on down the tunnel for the next shot. Zack, do you remember how David captured the city of Jerusalem?"

I thought, but I couldn't remember.

Dr. Doone didn't explain then, but when the video camera was ready again, he said, "David brought his men to this tunnel because of this shaft that led up to the city."

We shined the lights up into the shaft, but they didn't reach the top of it. Dr. Doone continued.

"David said, 'Whoever can get into the city first, and kill those blind and crippled guards, will be the captain of my army.' So Joab climbed up this shaft into the city and led the attack. David took the city and Joab became the captain of the army."

Ach and I wanted to try to climb up the shaft too. But Dad wouldn't let us. Still, it was neat to be right there where David and his men had been. It was definitely a good clue that the Bible story was true and that David was a real person.

So tonight we're staying in a hotel in Jerusalem and before I go to sleep, I'm writing down everything that happened today.

I've been thinking about what Dad said about believing that Mr. Roberts is the thief. I really do want to be like David and not like King Saul.

God, please put your footprint on me like you did on David. I want to be patient like he was, not quick to judge others like Saul was. Amen.

Now, it's time to think like a detective. If Mr. Roberts is not the thief, why is he on this trip with us? And why does he always disappear at the same time someone steals our things? The clues to solve this mystery are probably all right here in my notebook.

Discoveries and Clues

Words to Remember

Hazor, Megiddo, Gezer: Cities that Solomon rebuilt

Gateway: Big stone entrance to a city, usually with a wooden gate to open and close

Gihon: The springs that brought water to Jerusalem

Jebusites: People who lived in Jerusalem before David captured it

Important Facts

First Kings 9:15 says that Solomon rebuilt Hazor, Megiddo, and Gezer. Archeologists have found gateways built in Solomon's time at each of those cities.

The shaft that David's men used to sneak into Jerusalem and capture it is still there. It's just like the Bible story says.

MRH Clues

I'm not going to judge Mr. Roberts anymore. I'll go back and think about the clues again.

ELEVEN

Writing on Rocks

At the pool of Gibeon

We started this morning in the car (as usual), so Stef and Ach decided it was time for a soccer lesson again.

"When the ball is near the goal, I try to kick it in," Stef said. "And if Ach is the goalie, he tries to stop it."

"Stuf is right," Ach started to say.

"My name isn't Stuf," Stef interrupted.

Ach went on. "I can catch the ball with my hands when I am the goalie," Ach added. "But only while I am in the goal box."

That sounded strange to me. "The goalie can catch the ball with his hands if he's standing in a box?"

Stef gritted her teeth. "The goalie box is the area in front of the goal. It's marked with lines so it's called a box."

Ach spoke up. "And the halfbacks help the goalie

93

protect the goal. But they can't use their hands."

"What if they are in the goalie box?" I asked.

Poof. Stef's hair flew while she answered. "It doesn't matter. Only the goalie can use his hands. If someone else touches the ball with her hands, it's a penalty."

"Oh, I know about penalties," I said. "How many yards do they have to back up?"

Ach looked at Stef like I was crazy again. "No, no," Stef shouted, "it's not American football. A penalty means that the other team gets the ball and a free kick from that spot. And if the penalty is near the goalie box, they try to score."

"Oh, I see," I said. "It's like a field goal. How many points do they get if they kick it over the goal posts?"

It's a good thing Dr. Doone interrupted us then. I think Stef was going to pull her hair out. Or mine.

"Before we get where we are going this morning," he said, "I want to tell about one or two places we won't be able to go. Zack, will you find 1 Kings 16 in your Bible?"

I did.

"Who became king of Israel in verse 22?"

I read it. "Omri became king. Who was he?"

Dr. Doone laughed. "If you read down to verse 28, you'll see that the next king of Israel was his son, Ahab.

Do you remember Ahab?"

Stef answered. "He was the wicked king married to Jezebel. They lived in the days that Elijah prayed and fire came down from heaven."

"Right," Dr. Doone said. "Now 2 Kings 3"—he paused while I turned to that chapter—"tells us that when Ahab died, his son took over and the king of Moab rebelled against him. Who does it say was the king of Moab?"

I read verse four. "King Mesha was king of Moab. Why does he matter?"

Dr. Doone handed me my notebook. "He matters because of thirty-two lines of writing carved into a stone found in Moab. Those lines tell the same story as the Bible. They say that Omri, king of Israel, conquered the country of Moab. But after Omri's son Ahab died, the king of Moab, named Mesha, rebelled."

I was impressed. "That's exactly what the Bible says."

Dr. Doone went on. "Some people doubted that a king named Omri ever really existed. The Moabite Stone was the first place outside of the Bible an Israelite king's name was found. Since then, eleven more kings' names have been found in other places."

I wrote it all down. "That's a great clue that the

Bible stories really happened."

"And that the people in the Bible were real people like us," Stef added.

"Oh," Dr Doone added, "since we mentioned Ahab, there's one more thing you might find interesting. The prophet Amos, who spoke for God during Ahab's days, talked about how badly the rich people like King Ahab were treating the poor people. In Amos 3:15, he talks about how God will destroy their fancy houses decorated with ivory."

"What is ivory?" Ach asked.

"It's what elephant tusks are made of," I answered. "People carve the white ivory into fancy statues or jewelry."

Dr. Doone said, "When archeologists found the palace of Ahab in Samaria, it was one of the few places in all of Israel where they found artifacts made of ivory."

This notebook is filling up fast.

When we got here to the site of Gibeon, Mr. Roberts helped Dad carry the video camera and stuff. I noticed that Dad carried the camera bag himself. Ach and I followed along behind, keeping an eye on Mr. Roberts and anyone else who looked suspicious.

"Ach, look at that guy in the dark blue robe. Did you see him near the car when we parked?"

Ach shook his head. "I don't remember him."

We watched as Dr. Doone began his talk near a big hole lined with rocks. "This is the famous pool of Gibeon. In 2 Samuel 2, you can read the strange story of a fight here between twelve of Joab's men and twelve of Abner's men. It seems that they all stabbed each other with swords at the same time and all died. And it all happened here at this pool."

Ach and I walked around it. The pool, now just an empty hole, was more than thirty-five feet across. It was about thirty feet deep, but stone steps wound around down to the bottom. We were about to start walking down when Stef ran up behind us.

"Look," she said, pointing across the pool toward Dad and Dr. Doone. They were talking and pointing down into the pool. The camera bag and stuff was behind them, and someone was moving closer to it.

"Ach! Isn't that the guy in the dark blue robe?"

"Yes. What do we do? He could be trying to steal the camera bag."

Stef said, "If we shout to your dad and he looks this way, that man could grab the camera bag and run."

"But if we don't do something, he may grab it and run anyway." I tried to think. "If we could throw something behind them, it would make them turn around. But all I have is my camera," I said, touching the case hanging from my neck.

Stef pulled an apple out of her bag. "Here, throw this. It was for my lunch."

I handed it to Ach. "You're the best pitcher we have. Try to throw it over their heads so it lands behind them near the camera."

"Hurry," Stef hissed. "That guy's getting closer."

Ach swung his arm and the green apple flew high into the air. We watched the apple soar over Dad's head and splat right behind him. Dad and Mr. Roberts jumped and spun around. The man in the dark blue robe jumped back, then turned and rushed away.

They were still looking around when we rushed up, but I noticed that Dad had the camera bag in his hands now. We explained about the apple. "When you turned around, he rushed off in that direction," I said as I pointed.

"Describe him for me," Mr. Roberts said. Stef and Ach told him about the dark blue robe and everything while I talked to Dad.

"I'm sorry we had to startle you with that apple. I knew Ach could throw it without hitting anyone. "

Dad looked at the splattered mess on the ground. "I think you did the right thing. That was quick thinking,

Zack. I'd better keep one hand on this bag. It sure is attracting a lot of attention."

"I guess I can't suspect Mr. Roberts this time," I said. "He wasn't the one trying to get the bag."

Dad was quiet for a minute while he watched Mr. Roberts talk to Ach. "Keep your eyes open. After all, he could have been keeping me busy so someone else would have a chance to grab it."

I hadn't thought of that. But I thought about it the rest of that day.

Discoveries and Clues

Words to Remember

Gibeon: The city that the Bible says had a famous pool or well

Omri: King of Israel

Mesha: King of Moab

Ivory: Elephant tusks, sometimes carved into jewelry or decorations

Samaria: City where Ahab had his palace

Important Facts

Some people doubted that King Omri really existed. Then a carved stone found in Moab told the same story as the Bible. It said that Omri conquered Moab and that Mesha rebelled against a king later.

The book of Amos talks about Ahab's rich houses decorated with ivory. And one of the few places in Israel where ivory has been found is the site of Ahab's palace.

The pool of Gibeon, the place where a very strange battle was fought, has been dug out. It's big.

MRH Clues

A man in a dark blue robe tried to steal the camera bag. Mr. Roberts was right there. Was he trying to help us find the thief, or trying to keep Dad busy so someone else could steal it?

TWELVE

Trapping a Thief

Near Jerulasem

This morning, we drove to the site of the ancient town of Lachish (lake-ish). Dr. Doone told us about it along the way. "Lachish was an important city after the days of David and Solomon. I'm sure you remember the story of King Hezekiah. The Assyrians were threatening to destroy Jerusalem, so Hezekiah asked the prophet Isaiah what to do."

"I remember," I said. "Isaiah told the king not to worry, that the Assyrians wouldn't take Jerusalem."

"Right. Well, the Assyrians, with King Sennacherib (sin-ack-er-rib) were attacking all the cities of Judah. The last and biggest of the cities that he destroyed was Lachish. We know, because archeologists found scenes from these battles carved in stone in Sennacherib's palace."

Ach asked, "Who is this Snacky Rib king?"

"He was the king of the Assyrians at that time."

I had a question. "Did those carved pictures give the names of the cities being attacked?"

"Yes, they did," Dr. Doone answered. "One scene is supposed to be the surrender of the city of Lachish. We'll see some of the evidence of that battle when we get there."

"What about Jerusalem? Why didn't he attack Jerusalem?" Stef asked.

"A monument from Sennacherib's palace tells that story. It says that he forced Hezekiah to send him money and riches, including thirty talents of gold. Zack, look up 2 Kings 18:14 and see what the Bible says about the same story."

I found it and read. "It says that Hezekiah was forced to give him three hundred talents of silver and thirty talents of gold. Just like old Snacky Rib's monument."

Dr. Doone went on. "Thirteen years later, Hezekiah refused to pay anymore and Sennacherib attacked again. Hezekiah asked Isaiah what to do again. Isaiah's answer is in 2 Kings 19:32 and 33."

I looked it up. "He said that the king of Assyria wouldn't attack Jerusalem but would leave and go home."

"That's exactly what happened. And do you remember

why? Look in verse 35.”

"The angel of the Lord killed 185,000 Assyrians in their camp. So Snacky Rib went home," I said. "Does the Assyrian monument tell about that?"

"No," Dr Doone answered. "But the Bible also tells how Sennacherib died. The next verses there say that he was worshiping at his temple and two of his sons attacked and killed him. And the Assyrian monuments agree with the Bible completely."

I started writing. "Well, if everything else the Bible says about the Assyrians turned out to be true, then that part of the story must be true too."

At Lachish, we filmed in front of the old city gate. "This is where the main battle was fought," Dr. Doone said to the camera. "While digging this area out, archeologists found real slings and sling stones used in the battle."

We wandered around and I took a few pictures with my camera. I still couldn't zip the case back up all the way when I put the camera inside.

Later, back at the hotel, Ach and Stef and I talked while we ate supper. "We have to figure out if Mr. Roberts is the thief. Let's look at the clues." I got out my notebook.

Stef said, "He's always around when something happens. I think he's involved somehow."

"He wasn't the one trying to steal the camera bag yesterday," Ach said. "It was someone else."

"Maybe," I said. "He could have been trying to keep Dad busy so his friend could grab it. But let's start at the beginning. Has anything actually been stolen? Besides my bag of clothes. I'm sure no one would steal that on purpose."

"Well, not really anything of ours. But remember the Egyptian police said that someone stole that golden cat statue," Stef said.

"But if Mr. Roberts and his friends stole that statue, what do they want with our camera bag?" I asked.

"The camera is worth a lot of money." Ach shrugged his shoulders.

I went over everything we had written down about Mr. Roberts. "He was doing something strange when the Egyptian police stopped us. He was sneaking around while we were in the desert, like he was trying to contact someone."

"Like maybe his fellow thieves," Stef said.

"He said he was chasing whoever stole my bag. He asked about the camera bag. He disappeared when some-one stole the car, but he seemed sure that it would return soon. And it did." I scratched my head with the pencil. "It doesn't add up. Sometimes, he seems to be helping us and sometimes he seems to be sneaking around."

Then a great idea hit me like a ton of bricks. "Let's set up a trap! Come on, I'll show you what we'll do."

A little later, we stood outside by the open trunk of the car. I lifted the camera bag up onto the car roof. "Are you sure this will work?" Stef whispered.

"Just do it the way we planned," I hissed back. Out loud, I said, "Well, I guess I have everything. Let's go back in."

"OK," Ach said loudly. "I'll be sure everything is locked up." Then he slammed the truck lid and we walked back toward our hotel room door.

"Don't look back," I whispered. Finally, we were inside with the door shut. "Keep the lights off." We crowded by the window and peeked through the blinds.

"Tell me how this plan works again, Zock," Ach said as we watched the camera bag on the car roof.

I explained again. "We took the camera out of the bag and filled the bottom with that really white sand from the hotel rock garden. Then I cut a hole in the bottom of the bag with my knife. Now, if whoever is trying to steal it is watching as close as I think they are, they will see it and think we forgot and left it on the car roof."

"So they will steal it. Won't that make your dad unhappy?" he asked.

"Well, yes, but this time, we'll be able to follow them even if the thief doesn't leave footprints. Because the sand will be falling out and it will leave a trail wherever the thief goes."

We watched quietly for a few minutes. I was still thinking about Mr. Roberts. "Stef, so you remember what Mr. Roberts said to us that night we trapped Ach? He told us to let him know if we saw anything else, but how did he say it?"

She thought. "He said to report anything unusual to him."

"That's right," I exclaimed. "He said to report it. Like he was a general in the army or someone that people report to. And Ach, what did he say to you guys yesterday after we scared off that thief with the apple?"

Now it was Ach's turn to think. "He said 'Describe him for me.'"

"Describe him," I thought out loud. "That sounds like...hey, I know what that sounds like! He's a..."

"Shhh! Look, someone's coming," Stef whispered. We held out breath and watched someone move swiftly out of the shadows, grab the camera bag and disappear into the darkness.

"Let's go," I shouted.

"Wait." Stef grabbed my arm. "You promised your dad

you'd tell him before you did anything like this again."

"That's what I meant," I said. "Let's go get Dad and follow the thief." We ran next door and burst into the room. "Come on, we can catch the thief," I shouted. "Let's go!"

Of course, we had to explain first. But in just a minute, we were all outside with flashlights, searching for the white sand trail. " Here it is," Ach shouted. "This way."

We followed it across the parking lot. Suddenly, the trail turned and went straight to one of the hotel room doors. "What do we do now?" I asked.

"I say we call the police," Dr. Doone said. Just then the door opened. And right there, holding the bag, was Mr. Roberts.

"Well, you're already here. Come on in," he said quickly. "I was just going to get you."

"I find that hard to believe," Dr. Doone said, as we all filed into the room.

"So you really are the thief," Dad said. "I'm sorry to see it. I'm calling the police."

"Wait," I said. "He's not the thief." Everyone turned and looked at me.

"Zack, he's holding the bag," Stef pointed out.

"He's not the thief," I repeated. "He's the police."

Now they just stared. "I just figured it out a few minutes ago. That's why he's been chasing after the thief. That's how he knew our car was coming back quickly. He'd already found it."

Mr. Roberts nodded. "Zack's right. But how did you figure it out?"

"It was the way you talked. 'Report to me,' you said, and 'Describe him.' You sounded just like the police on TV."

He shook his head. "Let me explain from the beginning. I work for an international division of the police that protects the archeology treasures of this whole area."

"Like a spy," Stef said, fluttering her eyelashes.

"Like you heard," Mr. Roberts went on, "someone stole a golden statue of a cat from a site in Egypt. We were closing in on the thief when they ran into you at the pyramids. They were seen dropping the cat into your camera bag."

"Why would they do that?" Dr. Doone asked, sitting down as if he was suddenly very tired.

"It's a common trick. That way, they can't be caught with it. They could always try to steal it back later."

"That explains why everyone's been after the camera bag," Dad said, sitting on the bed.

"We weren't sure at first that you weren't one of the

smugglers. So I disguised myself as a tourist and followed you until I knew that you weren't aware of the cat."

"I saw you," I said. "That's when I became suspicious."

Mr. Roberts laughed. "I joined your group so I could catch the thieves trying to steal the cat statue back."

"What about when the Egyptian police stopped us?" I asked. "Was that some kind of signal?"

"You're right again, Zack. Those police were told to skip the car with my red hat on the seat. I didn't want them finding the cat. The rest of the time, I was trying to catch the thieves. I almost did twice. I missed the car thief by just a few seconds. He abandoned the car a few miles away."

"Wow," I sighed. "And I thought you were the thief. By the way, how did you get the camera bag? And where is the cat statue?"

He held up the bag. Sand was still pouring out of the hole. "This was a good idea. We were watching too. When the thief grabbed it, we grabbed him and brought him here. My driver is already taking him to the local police station. As for the cat, I don't know. I have to admit that one of the first things I did when I joined you was to search the camera bag. But it wasn't there."

Dad looked at Dr. Doone. They both shook their

heads. "We haven't seen it."

"This part of the case puzzles me." Mr. Roberts said. "Obviously, the thieves thought the cat was still in your bag. That's why they kept trying to steal it. We may never know what happened to it."

I sat down on the floor and my camera case hit me right on the knee. "Ouch," I mumbled. Then I shouted, "Wait! I know where the golden cat is!"

Discoveries and Clues

Words to Remember

Lachish: An important city in Hezekiah's days

Sennacherib: King of Assyria

Assyria: Country near Israel

Talents: Measures of gold or silver, like a pound or an ounce

Important Facts

The Bible story of Lachish being captured by Sennacherib was found carved in pictures on the walls of Sennacherib's palace.

A monument found in the palace says that Hezekiah had to pay Sennacherib thirty talents of gold. So does 2 Kings 18:14.

The Bible tells how Sennacherib died. Writing found on Assyrian monuments agree with the Bible story.

MRH Clues

Boy, was I wrong at first. But I think I figured it out. It's a good thing I wrote down all the clues.

THIRTEEN

The End of the Trip

I carefully unzipped my camera case and took out the camera. Then I reached in and pulled out the golden cat statue.

"Zack! How did you get it?" Everyone seemed to ask at once.

"Remember, Dad, I kept my camera in your video camera bag until we put a strap on it so it could hang around my neck. I had my camera out most of the time we were at the pyramids, but I left the case in your bag. The cat must have fallen into my camera bag when they dropped it in yours."

Stef rubbed her head. "That explains this knot. I knew there was something hard in that little bag."

"And that's why it didn't want to zip up right," Ach said with a smile.

I handed the statue to Mr. Roberts. "Take good care of it."

"Thank you, Zack. You're quite a detective," he said. "You know, when I joined your group, I really didn't think the Bible stories were true. But now, after seeing all the things we saw, and spending time with you people, I'm changing my mind."

We all had to smile about that.

Just a few days later, we had to pack and leave for home. When I told Ach goodbye, he promised to write and teach me more about soccer. I promised to look for him again if we ever come back. I'll have to ask Dad if Ach can come and visit us next summer.

When I told Stef goodbye (no mushy stuff!), she said her family was traveling to the United States soon and that she might stop and see me. Then, with one last poof, she was gone.

Dr. Doone sat next to me and talked for a while. "Well, Zack, what about your Bible clues? Do you think there's enough evidence that the Bible stories are real?"

"Oh, yes," I answered. "More than I imagined. There's more than enough reasons to believe that the people the Bible talked about really were alive. Especially since people in other countries wrote about them too. Thanks for taking me along."

"I'm glad you got to see it, Zack. I hope you never forget that the Bible is real and that God is real. And that means he really loves you, just like the Bible says."

Dad came and sat in the seat next to mine for our supper. If you could call it that. I hope no one ever invites me out to eat on an airplane. Anyway, while we ate, we talked.

"Zack, I was proud of the way you figured out the mystery of the thieves and the golden cat statue. And that you didn't judge Mr. Roberts before you had all the facts."

I blushed a little. "Thanks, Dad. I decided that you were right and that I wanted to be like David, not like Saul. I want God to put his footprint on me."

Dad patted my arm. "Good. Did you get to see everything you wanted to see?"

"Almost everything. Maybe when we go back..."

He laughed. "Don't count on it. Your mother may never let us out of her sight again. So tell me, what's the most important thing you learned?"

I had to think about that. "I always thought that the clues that the Bible is true came from digging up old cities or visiting famous places. But I learned that the best evidence that the Bible is real is in people."

"You mean people like Joshua and David and Moses?"

"Yes. The way they lived showed that they knew God

and that he was working to change them. But it's true about us, too. If the Bible is true, if God is real, then we should be different too. We should be kind and honest and patient all the time, when we're playing baseball or going to school or going to church. Other people should be able to see God's footprints on us."

Dad smiled a big smile. "I knew it was a good idea to bring you on this trip. You really have learned a lot." We sat quietly for a while, then he took a drink of his orange juice and made a face. "I don't know about you, Zack, but I will be glad to get home."

I looked at my plate and nodded.

"Why don't you take a nap when you're through eating. It's still three or four hours until we land. And your mom is going to want to hear all about our trip when we get home."

I think I will sleep after I finish writing this. It will be nice to be home. I just hope Mom has a full jar of peanut butter.

Red Hat Mystery

Spiritual Building Block: Acceptance

You can become less judgmental in the following ways:

Think About It:

Can you think of someone who doesn't like you? Does it ever make you angry or sad that she feels this way about you? Don't you wish that she would just listen to your side of the story, that she would try to understand you better? If only she knew you better, maybe she wouldn't be so mean. Is there someone that you don't like, that you might enjoy more if only you knew him better?

Talk About It:

Next time you feel angry or frustrated with someone, take some time to try to understand her. Find a friend or family member who speaks kindly of people; ask him to help you come up with as many reasons as possible why the person you are frustrated with acts the way she does. Once you put yourself in her place, you will find it easier to forgive her.

Try It:

If you meet a person who scares you a little bit because he is so different from you, make a decision to be brave. Introduce yourself in a kind way and then ask him about himself: What is his favorite sport? What does he do after school? How many brothers or sisters does he have? Chances are you'll find a person who is much like you no matter how different he looks. And you just might make a new friend.

Detective Zack:
Secret of Noah's Flood

"Nobody believes Noah and his flood is a true story!" At least that's what Zack's friend Bobby says. What do you believe? Discover the truth about Noah's flood in this action-packed story that will capture your imagination while it builds your faith in the Bible.

ISBN: 0-78143-730-X....................Retail Price: $5.99

Detective Zack:
Mystery at Thunder Mountain

A "tribe" of unbelievers, strange cries in the night, large footprints in the canyon, and a series of thefts have Zack and Kayla searching for answers at Thunder Mountain Camp. Who is taking the horses out of the corral at night, and why? The list of suspects is growing longer every day. Everything is not what it seems at this summer camp.

ISBN: 0-78143-731-8....................Retail Price: $5.99

Detective Zack:
Danger at Dinosaur Camp

Huge, unexplained footprints in the canyon, reports of a long-necked creature roaming the mountain, loud cries in the night! It can't be a living dinosaur—or can it? Could a dinosaur be at the bottom of all the strange happenings in Dinosaur National Monument? That's what Detective Zack is going to find out.

ISBN: 0-78143-732-6....................Retail Price: $5.99

Detective Zack:
Missing Manger Mystery

Mrs. Hopkins warned that disaster was certain if the church Nativity scene were held outdoors. Truer words were never spoken! A fire nearly destroys the stable, and Mrs. Hopkinsí 80-year-old manger from Bethlehem is missing. Zack and his friend Luke chase the clues that eventually lead them to the villain and the true meaning of Christmas.

ISBN: 0-78143-789-X....................Retail Price: $5.99

Detective Zack:
Secrets in the Sand

Zack and his father are on a learning trip to the Middle East. As they visit pyramids, historical cities, and archaeological sites, they learn more about the people described in the Bible. As evidence to support the Bible stories grows, so do the questions. Join Zack and his friends on a search for truth.

ISBN: 0-78143-803-9...................Retail Price: $5.99